W9-DAX-735

WITHDRAWN

EYE TO EYE
with Cats

Persian Cats
Lynn M. Stone

ROURKE PUBLISHING
Vero Beach, Florida 32964

www.rourkepublishing.com

PHOTO CREDITS: © Andreea Manciu: 8; © Suzanne Mulligan: 9; © Burak Demir: 14; all other photos © Lynn M. Stone

Editor: Jeanne Sturm

Cover and page design by Heather Botto

Library of Congress Cataloging-in-Publication Data

Stone, Lynn M.
 Persian cats / Lynn M. Stone.
    p. cm. -- (Eye to eye with cats)
 Includes index.
 ISBN 978-1-60694-334-2 (hard cover)
 ISBN 978-1-60694-860-6 (soft cover)
1. Persian cat--Juvenile literature. I. Title.
 SF449.P4S762 2010
 636.8'32--dc22
                                        2009005984

Printed in the USA

CG/CG

RouRke PuBLiSHing

www.rourkepublishing.com - rourke@rourkepublishing.com
Post Office Box 643328 Vero Beach, Florida 32964

Table of Contents

Persian Cats

Under that blanket of long fur and behind those big, bright eyes lurks the gentle Persian. The Persian's sweet nature and **unique** looks have made it the most popular of cat **breeds**.

The Persian's broad, flat face gives it the look of a **calm**, wise old owl—with fur.

The gentle Persian thrives in a peaceful environment.

The Persian's Looks

The Persian is not the only cat with long hair. It is the only breed, however, with long hair and a flat face.

The extreme Persian has an extremely flat face. The traditional Persian's face is not as flat. Traditional Persians are sometimes called *doll faces*.

Extreme Persian

Traditional Persian

Persians have round, **broad** heads. Many have gold eyes. Silver Persians have green eyes.

Persians have stocky bodies and short, sturdy legs. They come in a huge assortment of colors, from white to black, and dozens of mixed colors. The Himalayan, or Himalayan Persian, is a light colored Persian with dark **points**.

This young Persian's eyes will change color as she matures. It can take up to a year and a half for a Persian to develop its true eye color.

Purebred Persians

Cats whose parents are both of the same breed are **purebreds**. A purebred Persian kitten has purebred Persian parents.

The great majority of cats are not purebreds. But cat **fanciers** like the fact that purebreds are usually **predictable** in both body and **temperament**.

Persian kittens are playful and affectionate, and they grow up to be docile companions, suitable for owners of all ages.

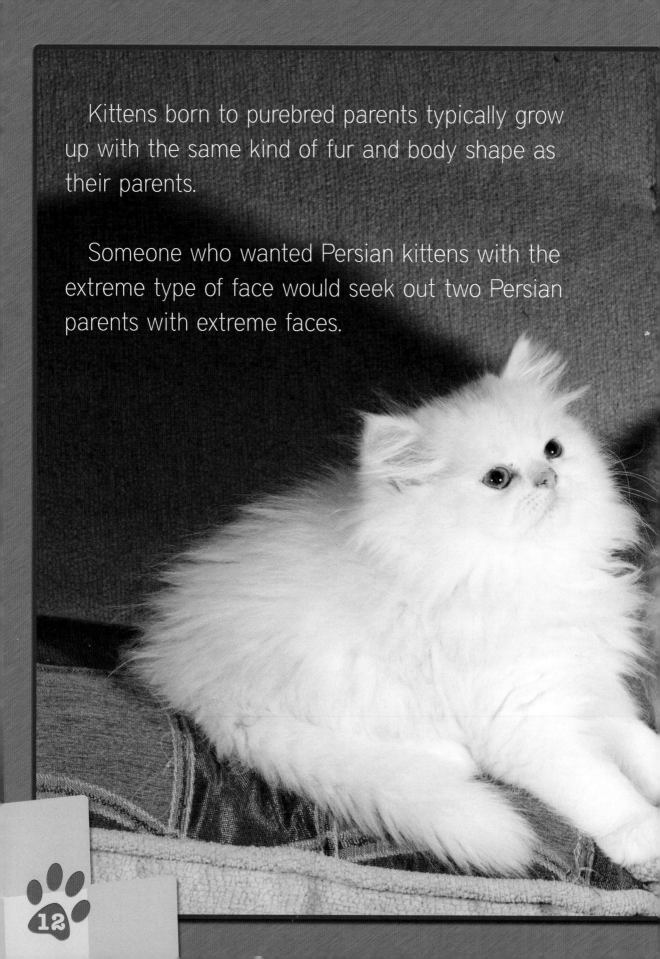

Kittens born to purebred parents typically grow up with the same kind of fur and body shape as their parents.

Someone who wanted Persian kittens with the extreme type of face would seek out two Persian parents with extreme faces.

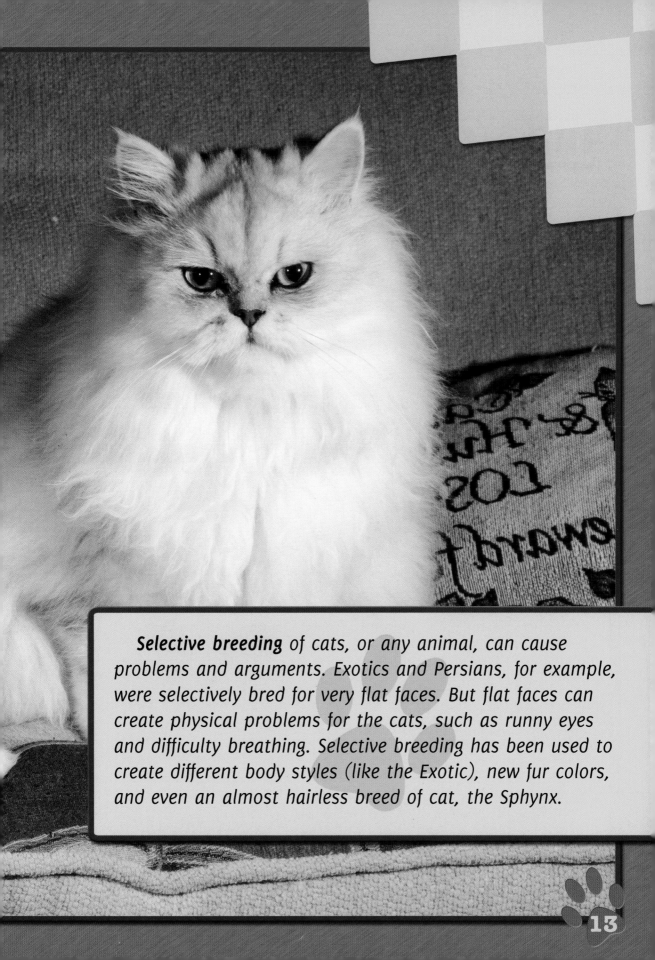

Selective breeding of cats, or any animal, can cause problems and arguments. Exotics and Persians, for example, were selectively bred for very flat faces. But flat faces can create physical problems for the cats, such as runny eyes and difficulty breathing. Selective breeding has been used to create different body styles (like the Exotic), new fur colors, and even an almost hairless breed of cat, the Sphynx.

The Cat for You?

The Persian has that remarkably unique look. And it has fur that would turn a red fox green with envy.

Keeping Persians indoors not only helps maintain a clean coat, it also protects the cats from disease and parasites.

It is a low energy cat. It is not built to run or jump particularly well. Most Persians prefer to just hang out and calmly study the world around them.

Persians are friendly, and in a quiet, undemanding way, they love attention from their human companions.

It's important to vaccinate cats to protect them from illness and to feed them the proper diet for each stage in their lives.

Not all cats like being groomed. Rewarding your cat with a special treat after grooming might make the task a little easier.

One type of attention a Persian needs is **grooming**. The long coat should be combed daily to prevent matting. Like other longhairs, Persians also need a bath now and then.

The History of Persians

The Persian is an old breed, but just exactly where and when it developed is a mystery. What is fairly certain is that a cat with long, thick fur somehow developed in Persia (now Iran) by the 17th century.

An Italian traveler, Pietro della Valle, first brought the breed to Europe, probably in the early 1600s. For the next two centuries, Persians were kept largely by the rich and famous. Persian cat fanciers were making the Persian popular in England and France.

Today, Persian cats are still the most popular breed of cat with Europeans and cat fanciers around the world.

By the late 1800s, as cat shows became popular, interest in the Persian spread rapidly.

Persians reached American shores at about the same time. The Persian quickly replaced America's own Maine Coon breed in popularity. And the Persian remains America's most popular purebred cat.

ABOUT CAT BREEDS

The beginnings of domestic, or tame, cats date back at least 8,000 years, when people began to raise the kittens of small wild cats. By 4,000 years ago, the Egyptians had totally tame, household cats. Most actual breeds of cats, however, are fewer than 150 years old. People created breeds by selecting parent cats that had certain qualities people liked and wanted to repeat. Two longhaired parents, for example, were likely to produce longhaired kittens. By carefully choosing cat parents, cat fanciers have managed to create cats with predictable qualities — breeds.

Persian Cat Facts

- 🐾 Date of Origin – unknown; before 1600
- 🐾 Place of Origin – Iran (Persia)
- 🐾 Overall Size – medium to large
- 🐾 Weight – 8-15 pounds (3.6-6.8 kilograms)
- 🐾 Coat – long
- 🐾 **Grooming** – daily
- 🐾 Activity Level – low
- 🐾 **Temperament** – affectionate; needs attention
- 🐾 Voice – quiet

Glossary

breeds (BREEDZ): particular kinds of domestic animals, such as Persian cats

broad (BRAWD): wide

calm (KAHM): peaceful, still

fanciers (FAN-see-erz): those who raise and work to improve purebred cats

grooming (GROOM-ing): the act of brushing, combing, and cleaning

points (POINTS): an animal's ears, face, tail, legs, and paws

predictable (pre-DIKT-uh-bul): that which can be decided before it happens

purebreds (PYOOR-bredz): animals with ancestors of the same breed

selective breeding (si-LEK-tiv BREED-ing): the process of carefully choosing parent animals so that a breed is gradually improved

temperament (TEM-pur-uh-muhnt): an animal's nature or personality

unique (yoo-NEEK): the only one of its type

Index

Websites to Visit

kids.cfa.org

www.ticaeo.com

www.cfainc.org/breeds/profiles/persian.html

About the Author

A former teacher and sports writer, Lynn Stone is a widely published children's book author and nature photographer. He has photographed animals on all seven continents. The National Science Teachers Association chose one of his books, *Box Turtles*, as an Outstanding Science Trade Book for 2008. Stone, who grew up in Connecticut, lives in northern Illinois with his wife, golden retriever, two cats, and abundant fishing tackle.